A Game for Jamie

Story by Maria McKernan

CHAPTER ONE

Jamie used to sit on the playground at recess. He liked to read his braille book. Sometimes he would listen to the sounds of the other children playing. He could identify the games they played. He liked softball best.

After recess, when the bell rang, the children would come to help Jamie back to the classroom.

They liked being with Jamie, but it was hard for him to join in all their games.

One day, a new boy named Paul started in Jamie's class. From his seat at the front, Jamie could hear Paul's loud voice coming from the back.

"If Paul doesn't watch out, he'll get in trouble," thought Jamie.

One recess, Jamie was eating his lunch when Paul sat down beside him and began to talk. He talked nonstop without taking a breath.

"What a motormouth," thought Jamie, smiling to himself.

9

"How much can you see?" Paul asked.

"He's nosy, too," Jamie thought.

"Just a little bit out of one eye," he told Paul. "More like a shadow, really. Nothing out of the other."

After lunch, they went outside to the playground. Paul said, "I'll go and play softball for a little while. Then I'll be back."

Jamie listened to the sounds of the children playing softball. He heard Paul's excited call of "You're out!" He wished he could play games.

11

CHAPTER TWO

The next day, Paul sat down beside Jamie and said excitedly, "I have something for you, Jamie. It's a ball with a bell inside."

"What would I want with that?" asked Jamie.

"You can learn to play softball. It's my baby sister's. I got the idea when I saw her chasing it. I thought, 'I'll take that for Jamie.' All you have to do is listen for the bell, then you'll know the ball is coming closer. Come on outside. Let's try."

Paul guided Jamie to a quiet corner of the playground and handed him a bat.

Jamie stood and listened. "I won't be able to do this," he thought nervously.

When he heard the bell coming closer, he swung the bat. The ball jingled past him, and Jamie's face fell.

"Never mind," called Paul brightly. "You'll get it. Now let's try again."

This time they moved over to the softball diamond.

Once more, Jamie lined up the bat and listened. Once more he missed. He tossed the bat onto the ground.

"It's no good," he said. "I'll never be able to hit the ball."

But Paul wouldn't let him give up. He made Jamie try again and again.

17

CHAPTER THREE

Jamie was suddenly aware of other voices urging him on, all shouting instructions at once:

"Move the bat back, Jamie."

"Bend your legs a little, Jamie."

"Here comes the ball, Jamie."

"Swing now!"

19

Jamie did. And he felt his bat make contact with the ball!

"I did it!" he cried, jumping up and down.

"Way to go, Jamie," replied Paul. Shouts and cheers sounded in Jamie's ears. It seemed to him as though the whole school had been watching.

"Let's all play softball," Jamie heard one of the children say.

"OK," they all said.

When Jamie hit the ball, Paul led him around the bases.

23

CHAPTER FOUR

"I'll teach you to play tennis, too, Jamie," said Paul as they walked back to class at the end of lunch recess.

Jamie smiled. He felt happy.

Soon Jamie was so busy he didn't have time to sit down at recess, except to rest between games.